The Snowman
The Book of the Film

RAYMOND BRIGGS

Pictures from the animated film THE SNOWMAN
selected by Taylor Grant

Puffin Books

PUFFIN BOOKS

Published by the Penguin Group
27 Wrights Lane, London W8 5TZ, England
Penguin Books USA Inc, 375 Hudson Street, New York, New York 10014, U.S.A.
Penguin Books Australia Ltd, Ringwood, Victoria, Australia.
Penguin Books Canada Ltd, 10 Alcorn Avenue, Toronto, Ontario, Canada M4V 3B2
Penguin Books (NZ) Ltd, 182-190 Wairau Road Auckland 10, New Zealand.

Penguin Books Ltd, Registered Offices: Harmondsworth, Middlesex, England.

First Published in Great Britain 1992 by Puffin Books

British Library Cataloguing in Publication Data
CIP data for this book is available from the British Library

ISBN 0-140-54800-9

Made and printed in Italy by Printers Trento srl

When James woke up it was snowing! He got dressed as quickly as he could and raced downstairs. "Don't forget your boots," said Mum. James tugged on his wellingtons by the front door. He couldn't wait to be out in the wonderful whirling snow.

In the garden James had a brilliant idea: he'd make a snowman! James rolled a snowball until it was almost up to his waist. He packed more snow round it until it was as tall as a man. Then he rolled another snowball for the head. The snowman shape was perfect, but there was something missing…

James rushed into the house. Mum gave him a woolly scarf and a hat, and James found a tangerine for the snowman's nose and lumps of coal for his buttons and his eyes. Then he drew a line for his mouth and the snowman was finished!

By now it was getting dark. "Tea-time," Mum called.
James said good night to the snowman and went slowly
back indoors.

 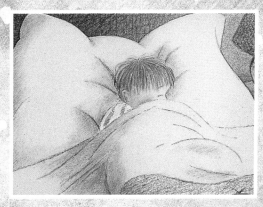 

Then it was time for bed. Mum kissed James good night and soon he was fast asleep.

When the grandfather clock struck twelve, James suddenly woke up. He went to the window and looked out at his snowman. He looked very lonely. James put on his dressing gown and tiptoed down the stairs.

James opened the front door without a sound.
When he stared out into the moonlit garden he could
hardly believe his eyes – the snowman moved!

He took off his hat politely and bowed. And then he started
to walk towards the house. James shook his hand.
"Would you like to come in?" he asked. The snowman
nodded.
"We must be very quiet," warned James, "or my parents
will wake up."

The snowman sat down in an armchair in the living room and stroked the cat sleeping by the fire. *Mrreaoowww!* His hand was freezing! The cat hissed and spat. The poor snowman nearly fell out of his chair with fright. James couldn't help laughing.

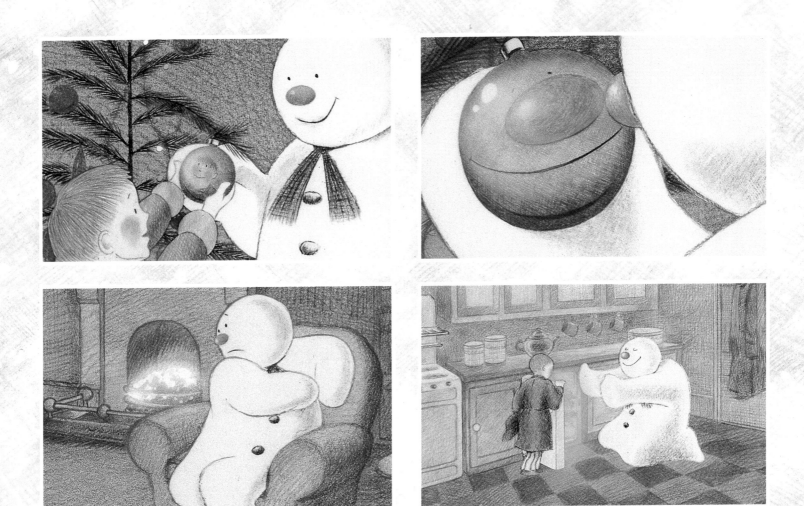

The snowman liked the Christmas tree – he could see his
face in the shiny decorations. But he was too close to the
fire and he had started to melt!

James took him into the kitchen and opened the fridge
door. The snowman looked much happier.

Whoops! Hot water isn't good for snowmen, either!
The snowman was thrilled to see a snowman on the
Christmas cake. The little model looked just like him.

Then the snowman found the fruit bowl and tried some new noses! He put on a pomegranate… a banana… even a pineapple. But the tangerine was still his favourite.

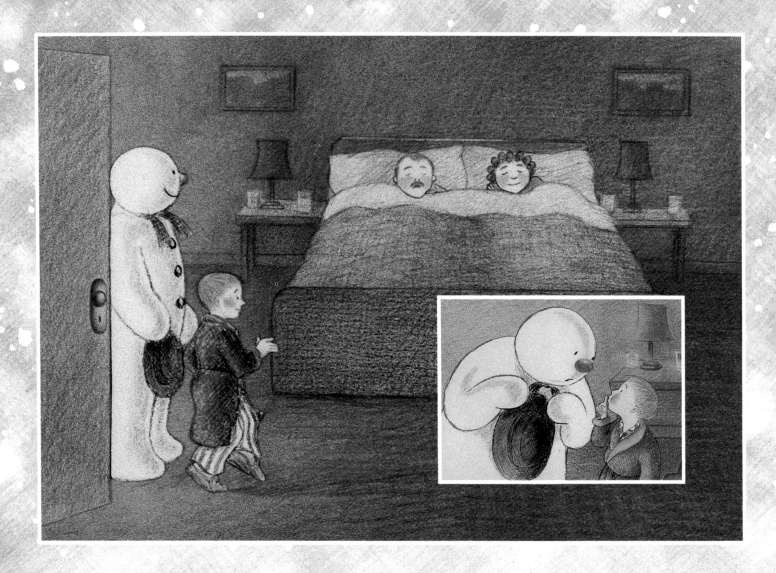

James took the snowman upstairs. "Ssshh! This is Mum and Dad's room," he whispered. The snowman wanted to have a closer look.

"Careful!" James just stopped the snowman from waking up his parents.

Dad's false teeth were a surprise! The snowman slipped them into his mouth and grinned.

The snowman gazed at a family photo. "Let's have a
dressing up game," whispered James. The snowman tried
out Mum's make-up and her best hat, put on Dad's
trousers and braces, and smoked Dad's pipe. "Try some of
Mum's perfume," said James.

Oh no! The snowman puffed Mum's perfume spray up his
nose by mistake! He could feel the most enormous sneeze
coming – "Aaaah… aaahh… aaa-tischoo!"

James took the snowman to his own room. The snowman found a musical box, wound it up and danced. Ooops! He trod on a rollerskate and fell over in a cloud of balloons. "Are you all right?" asked James. The snowman nodded.

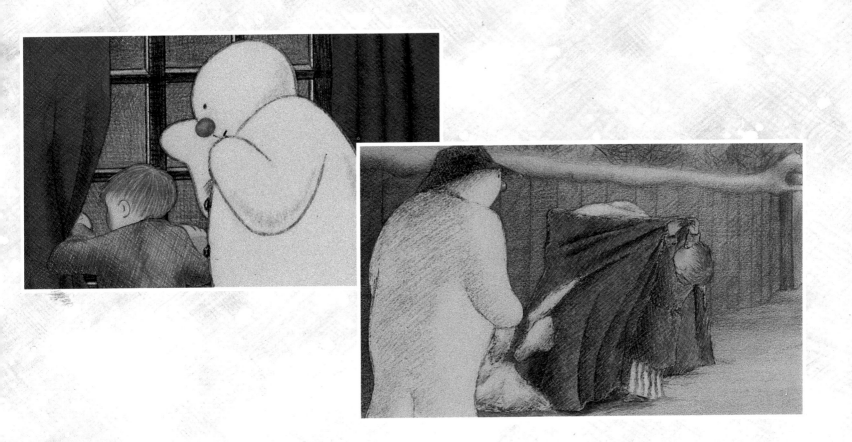

"Come on," said James. "I've another idea. We can go for a ride!" They tiptoed out into the open air to where a dark tarpaulin covered an old motorbike.

The snowman started the engine and turned on the
headlamp. "I'll hang on tight!" cried James, and the two of
them roared off through the snowy countryside, watched
by an owl and some inquisitive rabbits.

When they came back to the garden, the heat of the engine had made the snowman's legs feel weak. James took him to the freezer in the garage and soon the snowman's legs were as good as new.

As they walked back to the house, the snowman suddenly
stopped. He seemed to have remembered something. He
gripped James's hand and began to run across the garden,
bounding, jumping, leaping, until James found they were
flying!

They flew for miles in the icy air. "This way!" cried some of the snowman's friends, and soon they came to the coast and the dark, stormy ocean. A friendly whale waved his tail and blew them a greeting.

Then land was in sight again. Where could they be?

All around them was a great forest of pine trees laden with snow. There were even some penguins! They landed silently in the icy wilderness.

James could hear music ahead. The snowman pushed
aside some pine branches and led him into a clearing.
All the snowmen in the world had come to a party.
There was delicious food and a band was playing.
The snowmen began to dance – with James in
the middle!

James danced with snowmen from all over the world: from
Scotland, Texas, Switzerland, even China!

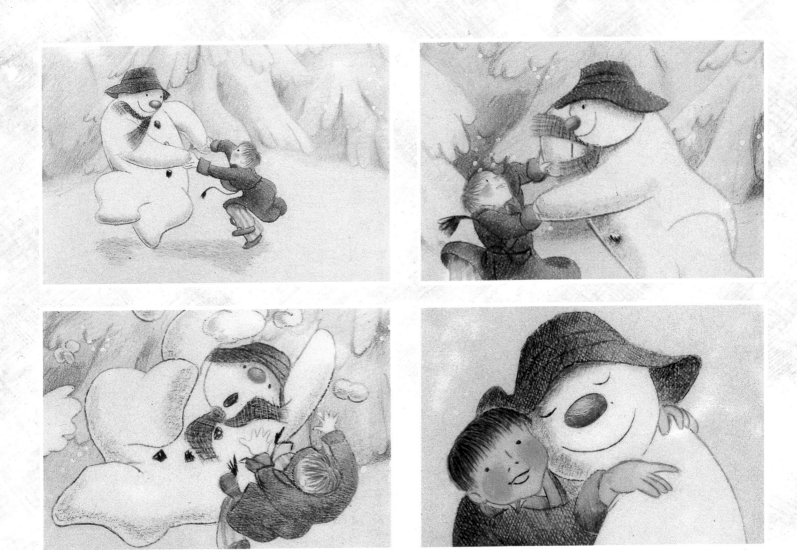

But his own snowman was best of all. They whirled and
twirled until they were giddy. Look out, James!
They tumbled over into the powdery snow. James gave
his snowman a big hug.

Guess who else was at the party: Father Christmas!
"I've got something for you, James," he said.
"Come with me."

Father Christmas rummaged among the presents. "This is the one!" he beamed. It was a beautiful blue scarf.

"Oh, thank you, Father Christmas," said James.

The snowman pointed at the moon sinking over the horizon. It was time to go.

Once again they flew through the frosty air until they saw James's house below. Skimming over the hedge, they landed back in the garden. James hugged the snowman. "It's been the best Christmas ever," he whispered. Then he walked back to the house, looking over his shoulder at the snowman.

The snowman waved goodbye. When James looked out of
his bedroom window he saw him standing in his old place
again. Tired and happy, James fell asleep.

When James woke up he remembered his wonderful
adventure. He rushed downstairs, ran past his parents
having breakfast and opened the door. The sun shone
warmly on his face.

But where was his snowman? An old hat, a scarf, some lumps of coal and a tangerine were lying on a pile of melted snow. Had it all been a dream? James felt the soft wool of the scarf in his dressing gown pocket. *He* didn't think so…